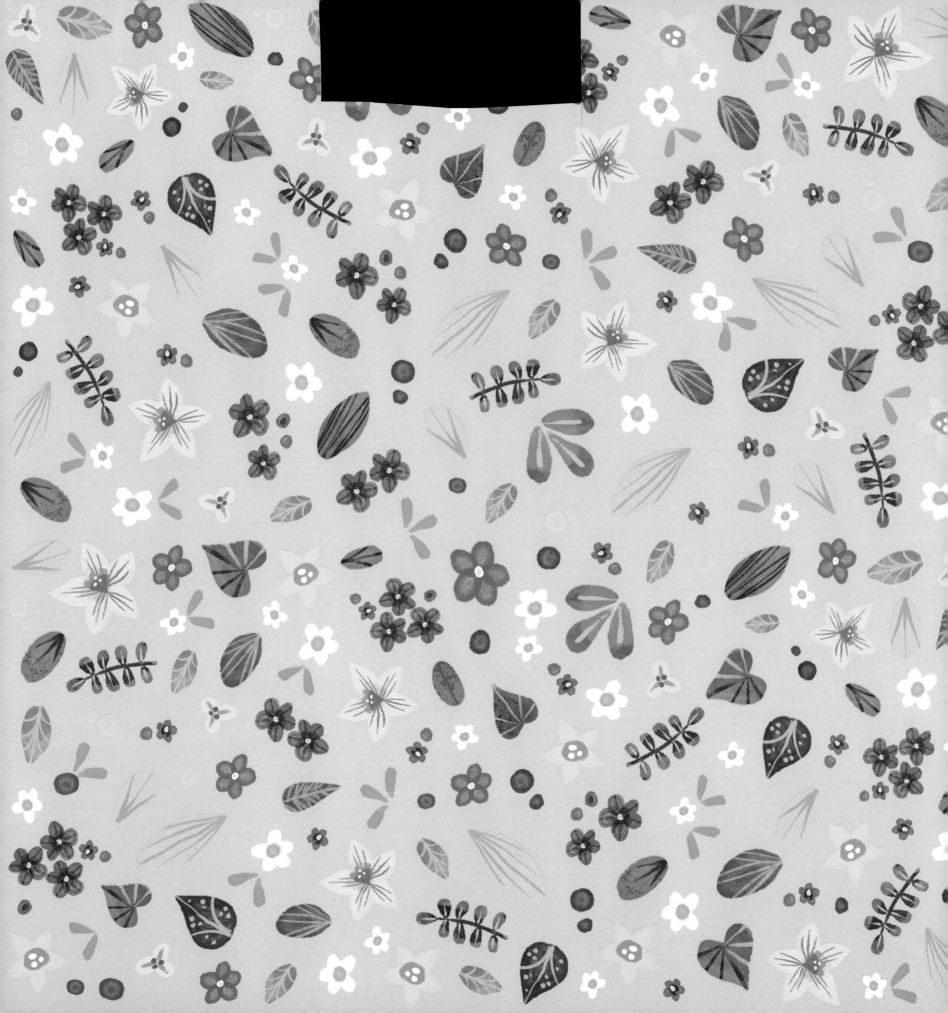

For Gran, with love x - LR

For my nephews - AC

First published 2018 by Macmillan Children's Books,
an imprint of Pan Macmillan
20 New Wharf Road, London N1 9RR
Associated companies throughout the world
www.panmacmillan.com

ISBN: 978-1-5098-4101-1 (HB)
ISBN: 978-1-5098-4102-8 (PB)
ISBN: 978-1-5098-8166-6 (EB)

Text copyright © Lucy Rowland 2018
Illustrations copyright © Anna Chernyshova 2018

1 3 5 7 9 8 6 4 2

A CIP catalogue record for this book is available from
the British Library.

Printed in China

Written by
LUCY ROWLAND

Illustrated by
ANNA CHERNYSHOVA

Catch that Egg!

MACMILLAN CHILDREN'S BOOKS

Floppit was a bunny with the most enormous feet,
His friends could hear him coming with his very bouncy beat.

He liked to skip,

he liked to hop,

he liked to
jump around,

And he loved the **BOINGY** noises
as he bounced along the ground.

But one day, in his burrow, as he hopped across the floor,
His mum said, **"STOP IT, FLOPPIT!** I can't take it anymore.

You're making such a racket! Can't you go outside to play?"
So Floppit thought, "I'll find my friends," and hopped off on his way.

But Chicken was too busy!
She was guarding lots of eggs,

When Floppit came a-jumping
on his long and hoppy legs.

"STOP IT, FLOPPIT!" Chicken said.
"Your noisy feet will shake them!
My eggs are very precious.
It's important not to break them."

Sheep was with her sleepy lambs, all curled up in the hay,
When Floppit came a-skipping and a-hopping up that day.
"STOP IT, FLOPPIT!" muttered Sheep.
"You're making such a din.

Hop off towards the cow shed now and see if Cow is in."

But Cow was with her baby calves and looked a little busy,
When Floppit came a-hopping by and left her feeling dizzy!

"STOP IT, FLOPPIT!" grumbled Cow.
"They're learning how to walk.

Your bouncing isn't helping and I haven't time to talk!"

So Floppit tried his other friends, but Dog and Cat and Pig Said, **"STOP IT, FLOPPIT!** Quiet now,

your feet are just too big!"

Floppit peered down at his feet, then slowly hopped away.
"Perhaps I'm just too bouncy. Oh, I only want to play."

It wasn't too long later that the bunny hopped along
And heard some noisy shouting.
"Oh!" he thought. "There's something wrong."

He stopped and watched and waited then he saw Cow running past,
Her calf had knocked poor Chicken's egg and . . .

off it rolled . . .

so fast!

The egg sped quickly down the hill and Cow ran right past Floppit.
"CATCH THAT EGG!" poor Chicken yelled, but no, Cow couldn't stop it.

The egg rolled past the big barn doors where Sheep stood, just inside.
"CATCH THAT EGG!" the cow cried out. "It's going to break!" she cried.

It rolled past Dog. It rolled past Cat. "**CATCH THAT EGG!**" Sheep said.

"**CATCH THAT EGG!**"

They yelled to Pig . . . it flew right past Pig's head!

The egg went up and up and then was falling through the sky,
But luckily the animals saw Floppit hopping by.
Such bouncy feet! Such hoppy legs! Was he the one to stop it?
They pointed up towards the egg and shouted . . .

Floppit crouched down really low
and with one mighty jump,

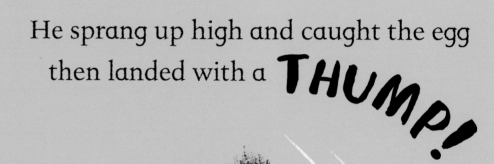

He sprang up high and caught the egg
then landed with a **THUMP!**

The friends all gave a great big cheer, the lambs began to bleat,
"Hip hip-hooray for Floppit and his very bouncy feet!"

Floppit felt so proud,
but then the egg began to
SHAKE!

He heard a little
CRACK!

and then the shell
began to
BREAK!

He rushed the egg to Chicken but he tripped up on his feet,
The egg flew slowly through the air and landed with a . . .

"TWEET!"

A head popped out,
    then two small legs,
    and Chicken shouted,
    "Quick!"

"CATCH IT FLOPPIT!"

laughed his friends.
"You've got to CATCH THAT CHICK!"

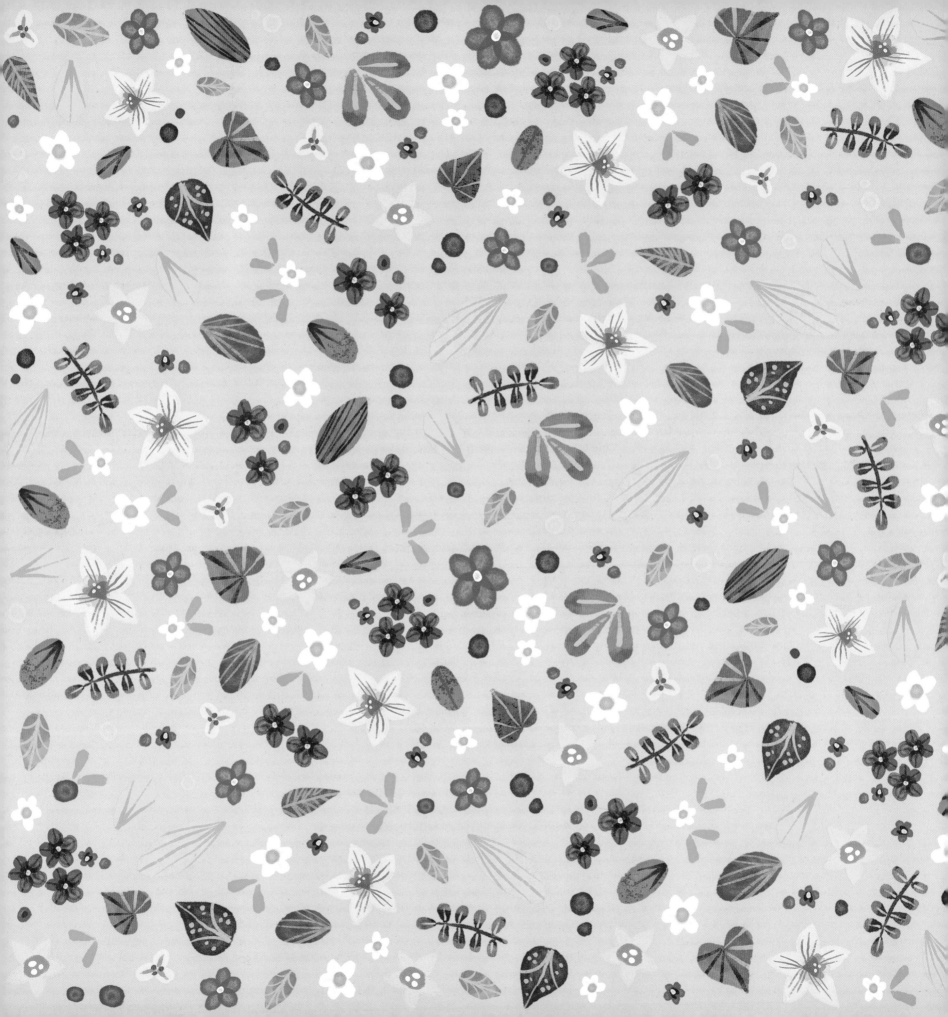